My Trucks

Note

Once a reader can recognize and identify the forty-two words used to tell this story, he or she will be able to successfully read the entire book. These forty-two words are repeated throughout the story, so that young readers will be able to recognize easily the words and understand their meaning.

The forty-two words used in this book are:

a	day	for	is	room	true
ahead	do	garbage	love	stuck	two
all	dream	get	mail	the	up
and	drive	I	my	there's	way
around	fast	if	on	to	you
car	fight	I'll	red	tow	you'll
come	fire	inside	rest	truck	your

Library of Congress Cataloging-in-Publication Data

Hall, Kirsten.
    My trucks / by Kirsten Hall; illustrated by Patti Boyd.
      p. cm. — (My first reader)
    Summary: While a little boy plays with his toy trucks, he imagines driving various real trucks such as a fire engine, a farm pickup, and an ice cream wagon.
    ISBN 0-516-05373-6
    [1. Trucks — Fiction. 2. Imagination — Fiction.] I. Boyd, Patti, ill. II. Title. III. Series.

PZ7.H1457My 1995
[E] — dc20

95–10106
CIP
AC

My Trucks

Written by Kirsten Hall   *Illustrated by Patti Boyd*

Children's Press®
A Division of Grolier Publishing
New York London Hong Kong Sydney
Danbury, Connecticut

4

I love to drive!

I drive a truck.

I'll tow your car if you get stuck.

I'll drive my truck

12

around all day.

14

I'll get your garbage on my way!

16

My fire truck is fast and red.

I'll fight the fire up ahead!

18

I drive a truck.

My dream come true.

Inside my truck is mail for you!

I love to drive my truck. I do!

You'll love my truck.

About the Author

Kirsten Hall was born in New York City. While she was still in high school, she published her first book for children, *Bunny, Bunny*. Since then, she has written and published fifteen other children's books. Currently, Hall attends Connecticut College in New London, Connecticut, where she studies art, French, creative writing, and child development. She is not yet sure what her plans for the future will be—except that they will definitely include continuing to write for children.

About the Illustrator

Patti Boyd was born in Columbus, Ohio. She now lives in Jackson Hole, Wyoming, with her daughter. Boyd has been a children's book illustrator for more than 20 years and is also Assistant Director at the National Museum of Wildlife Art. Boyd loves being near the mountains, and she enjoys hiking, cross-country skiing, and wildlife watching.